W9-DCD-779

Tillie & Clementine
Noises in the Night

By Dan Killeen

Happy Fun Books
St. Louis

Tillie & Clementine - Noises in the Night

Published by
Happy Fun Books
St. Louis, MO

Printed by
MCI Printing
St. Louis, MO

ISBN 978-0-9898474-0-7

www.TillieandClementine.com

To Mom and Dad

There once was a girl named Tillie and she had a sister named Clementine and they loved to have fun.

They lived with their parents in an old brick house down in Benton Park.
The houses in that neighborhood were really close together.

One night Mommy announced that she had to go to a neighborhood board meeting, leaving Daddy and the girls to fend for themselves.

But young Clementine voiced what everyone was thinking,
"Mommy no! Don't go to the bored meeting! Stay with us!"

"Oh Clementine, honey," said Mommy, "you will all be fine. Daddy will fix your dinner and get you ready for bed."

"Really??" Clementine questioned.

"Well, sure!" insisted Daddy, "I can handle things, girls. I'm a grown-up and an architect. We'll be okay."

Mommy told Tillie and
Clementine to be good
girls, eat what Daddy
makes for supper,
and clean their room
before bed.

After some hugs good-bye
she was off to her meeting.

7

"Okay, girls," Daddy said as he turned toward the kitchen, "let's go see what we can find in the fridge."

Daddy began scrounging for items which he could assemble into a proper meal. The girls took their places at the kitchen table and waited patiently.

Daddy pulled out all sorts of leftovers that had been hiding in the back of the refrigerator. He was determined to show the girls he could really whip up something special for supper.

They were not impressed with Daddy's efforts. "This looks yucky!" declared Clementine.

"Daddy, can we PLEEEASE have macaroni and cheese instead?" implored Tillie.

Daddy said, "Fine," and made the girls macaroni and cheese. He ended up eating the two meals he had prepared for them.

And there was contentment at the kitchen table.

"Alright," announced Daddy after they had their fill. "Time to get ready for bed." He scooped up the girls and climbed the staircase.

Since Tillie was a big girl she could get dressed for bed by herself, but young Clementine needed a bit of help. Daddy asked them, "Okay, you girls want me to read you a story or just make one up?"

"Make one up!" hollered Tillie.

Daddy plopped down in the chair and began his story...*There once was a girl named Tillie and she had a sister named Clementine and they loved to have fun.* He always began his stories that way.

15

Tillie and Clemmie were princesses in the Kingdom of Funlandia!
They lived in an old stone castle with their parents,
King Daddy-o the Awesome and Queen Mommy-o the Curly.

16

One day, the king and queen had to leave on an overnight trip to attend a royal board meeting. As they were pulling away the queen instructed her princess daughters, "Be good girls while we're gone and clean up your room." The king added, "Don't stay up late playing with your toys and don't eat too much dessert."

That night the girls stayed up late playing with their toys and eating lots of figgy pudding. They finally fell asleep leaving a mess of toys and pudding bowls all over their room.

18

What the girls didn't know was that lying in the nearby woods a big dragon had caught the scent of figgy pudding coming from the castle. It was his favorite dessert and he began to drool.

19

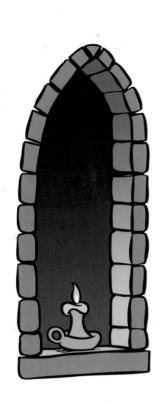

SCRATCH

OOMF

GRUNT

SNORT

Princess Tillie and Princess Clementine were soon awakened by strange, scary noises coming from just outside their window!

Tillie peeked outside to see what was making the terrible commotion.

21

"Oh no, Clementine! There's a big, ugly dragon crawling up the side of the castle!" shouted Tillie.

"Oh no!" cried Clementine, "What will we do?"

And the dragon scampered away and back into the woods. The girls had saved the castle!

HOORAY!

The next day King Daddy-o and Queen Mommy-o returned from their trip. The queen said, "Well girls, looks like you survived without us for a day and managed to clean your room."

And the king joked, "I'm just glad you didn't burn the castle down. Ho ho ho!"

Tillie winked at Clementine and Clementine giggled.

The End...

"Good story, Daddy!" declared Tillie from her bunk. "Yeah, good story," agreed Clementine.

"Thanks, girls," said Daddy, and he kissed them each good night. "Sleep well."

Daddy went back downstairs and, remembering that it was Tuesday night, realized he needed to take the recycling bin to the front curb. So he dragged the big green container out front into the cold night.

But when he returned to the front door he found it had locked behind him. He checked his pockets and recalled he'd left his keys inside. He ran around the house and tried the back door - locked as well!

Daddy's nose began to run as he struggled to think of a way back into the house.

28

GRUNT

SNORT

!

*

SCRATCH

OOMF

Clementine
was soon
awakened
by strange,
scary noises
coming from
just outside
her window.

29

Outside, Daddy was trying to shimmy his way up the side of the house by pressing himself against it and the house nextdoor.

Clementine jumped out of bed and screamed, "Tillie, wake up! There's a dragon outside our window trying to get in! What are we going to do?!"

OOMF

GRUNT

HEY, GIRLS!

Tillie rushed down from her bed and told Clementine, "Quick! Gather up all the toys and stuff from the floor and meet me by the window!"

"Okay, Tillie!" answered Clementine. "But I hear the dragon getting closer!"

Then the girls went to the window and chucked all of their toys and things at what they thought was a big, ugly dragon but was really just Daddy trying to get back inside.

Daddy fell back down to the ground and landed with a thud! The girls celebrated because they heard the crash and figured they had vanquished the dragon.

34

He stumbled back around to the front of the house, and by that time Mommy was just returning home from her meeting. She saw Daddy and said, "Hey, honey! Watch'ya doing out here?"

"Ughh," moaned Daddy, "I locked myself out."

Mommy had her keys, so they went inside and upstairs to check on the girls. She whispered to Daddy, "Great job, honey! They're fast asleep and you got them to clean up their room."

"Well," said Daddy, "they are our little princesses."

The End